Tell Somebody It Happened to Me

Nancy Flowers

WinePress **WP** Publishing Kids

To order additional copies of this title call:
1-877-421-READ (7323)
or please visit our Web site at
www.winepressbooks.com

If you enjoyed this quality custom-published book,
drop by our Web site for more books and information.

www.winepressgroup.com
"Your partner in custom publishing."

WinePress Publishing (PO Box 428, Enumclaw, WA 98022) functions only as book publisher. As such, the ultimate design, content, editorial accuracy, and views expressed or implied in this work are those of the author.

ISBN 13: 978-1-57921-977-2
ISBN 10: 1-57921-977-2
Library of Congress Catalog Card Number: 2008931858

Printed in South Korea.

My name is Jacob. I'm a kid just like you.
And sometimes we kids don't know what to do.

Big people don't always do what is right.

Sometimes they scare us, especially at night.

We all have privates—parts no one should touch.

Even big people who say, "I love you so much."

Sometimes their words don't match what they do.
By touching your privates, they're hurting you.

Just tell them no! Tell them, "That's bad!
I won't play that game, even if you look sad."

"I won't keep that secret, though you say I must.

I'm telling somebody—somebody I trust."

My privates are mine, no one else's to see.

My name is Jacob, and it happened to me.

What's your name? Has it happened to you?

No need to feel bad; now you know what to do.

It wasn't your fault; be brave and get free.
Tell somebody, "It happened to me."

To the parent/guardian—The purpose of this book is to teach children to tell someone if anyone touches them inappropriately. It is an opportunity to discuss which parts of their anatomy are private. The person most likely to sexually abuse your child is a person your child knows and trusts. Teaching your child to tell someone could spare him or her a lifetime of pain. The most effective prevention happens before a child is harmed. If inappropriate behavior is revealed, don't ignore the problem.

It wasn't your fault; be brave and get free.
Tell somebody, "It happened to me."

No need to feel bad; now you know what to do.

What's your name? Has it happened to you?

My name is Josie, and it happened to me.

My privates are mine, no one else's to see.

I'm telling somebody—somebody I trust."

"I won't keep that secret, though you say I must.

Just tell them no! Tell them, "That's bad!
I won't play that game, even if you look sad."

Sometimes their words don't match what they do.
By touching your privates, they're hurting you.

Even big people who say, "I love you so much."

We all have privates—parts no one should touch.

Sometimes they scare us, especially at night.

Big people don't always do what is right.

My name is Josie. I'm a kid just like you.
And sometimes we kids don't know what to do.

Tell Somebody It Happened to Me

Nancy Flowers

WinePress **WP** Publishing Kids